This is me.
I'm the one with the **pointy**
nose and **b e a d y** eyes.
The cutesy one
in the middle.

I live in
dustbin
number **3**,
Grubby
Alley.

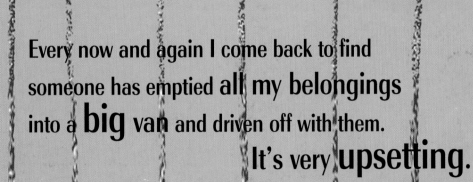

Every now and again I come back to find
someone has emptied **all my belongings**
into a **big** van and driven off with them.
It's very **upsetting**.

I'm a brown rat, a street rat.
But people call me that pesky rat.
I don't know why.
They say I smell,
but that's not my fault, it's the dirt.

Sometimes when I am tucked into
my crisp packet,
I look up at all the cosy windows
and wonder what it would be like
to live with creature comforts.
To belong to somebody.
To be an actual pet.

Most of all I would like

that
pesky
rat

Lauren Child

ORCHARD

Thank you
Randala
and Albena

Look out for Lauren Child's
Clarice Bean books
and the award-winning
I will not ever
NEVER
eat a tomato

Max

and for anyone who
has ever wished the
were somebody's p•

Sam

Lucy

Zaida

and for fabulous
Frances and her
pets Lucy, Sam,
Ata and Cui

Louie

This book is for
the gorgeous Max
and her little
dog Louie

Flame

Sita

Ata & Cui

Twinkle

with love to Jo and Thomas,
long-suffering owners of Twinkle,
the Bette Davis of cats

Cheeky

ORCHARD BOOKS
Carmelite House
50 Victoria Embankment
London, EC4Y 0DZ
ISBN 978 1 40833 737 0
First published in 2002 by Orchard Books
This edition published in 2016
Text and illustrations
© Lauren Child 2002, 2008
The right of Lauren Child to be identified
as the author and illustrator of this
work has been asserted by her in
accordance with the Copyright, Designs
and Patents Act, 1988.

A CIP catalogue record for this book
is available from the British Library.
10 9 8 7 6 5 4 3 2 1
Printed in China
Orchard Books is an imprint of Hachette Children's Group
Part of The Watts Publishing Group Limited
An Hachette UK company   www.hachette.co.uk
St Mungo's Broadway Registered Charity No 1149085
www.mungosbroadway.org.uk

Donut

to have a **name**, instead of just that *pesky rat.*

My friend Pierre,

who is a **chinchilla**, is looked after by a rich lady called Madame Fifi.

He has a very **glamorous** life.

He lives in the lap of luxury.

I say,
"I would quite like to
live in a fashionable apartment
and be fed
chocolates
while I sit on a
feather cushion."

I hate having baths.

I think I'm **allergic** to soap.

Then there's this **Siamese** cat called **Oscar**. He lives with **Mr Washington,** a **busy** businessman.

Mr Washington is **always** at **work** so he doesn't have time to **wash fur** or be **strict.**

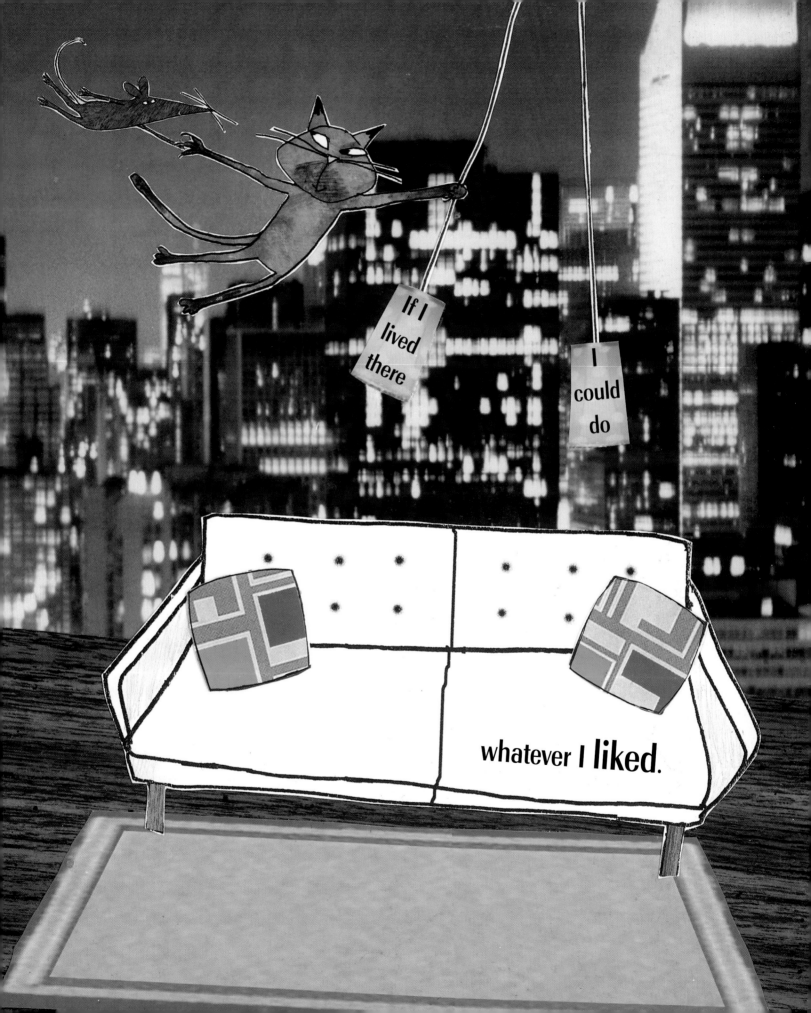

I'm quite good in the kitchen

but I hate to be bored.

Swinging on the trapeze one minute, tip-toeing on the high wire the next.

Nibbles says,
"It is fun hopping through hoops in a tutu.
But sometimes
I could do with
taking
off
the
clown's
nose
and putting my feet up."

Maybe it's all a bit ne rve wracking for me.

I think I'd quite like one of those owners
who do lots of **sitting about**
like **Miss StClair**.

Her **Scottie** dog, Andrew, is **always** sitting by the

fire, having **supper** on a tray and they spend the evenings doing **Puzzles** together.

Andrew says,

"On the whole I feel **very well** looked after.

And Miss StClair is good company.

But it's rather **embarrassing** when we go out shopping."

Miss StClair makes Andrew wear a little hat and coat.

So in the morning
I go to the pet shop
and ask Mrs Trill

if she has

an owner

who might want me.

She says, 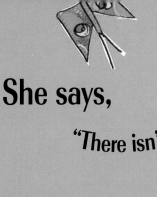  "There isn't much call for brown rats, and I'm afraid you aren't very **popular** with the public."

I say,  "I don't see why not. I'm very good **company**, always **popping up** when you least expect me to, and I am happy to eat **anything**, even if it's been slightly **nibbled**."

Mrs Trill says,   "Well, you could always make a **notice** and put it in the **window**. You never **know**."

So I write:

Me

Brown rat looking for kindly owner
with an interest in cheese
Hobbies include nibbling and chewing
would like a collar with my name on
would like a name
would prefer no baths
will wear a jumper if pushed
Yours Keenly
Brown rat (that pesky rat)

P.S sorry about bad paw writing

not
a very good picture

Anonymous

Then I wait   and   I   wait

and   I   wait.   Until . . .

. . . on Tuesday old Mr Fortesque is passing
and he **stops** to look at my **notice**.

He has to really **squint** because he
has such **bad** eyesight.

Then he looks at me and says,

"**My,**
haven't you
got a pointy nose
and, goodness me,
what a long tail, and such
unusual beady eyes . . .

I'll take him."

I can't
believe my **luck,**
nor can Mrs Trill.

Mrs Trill says,
"Are you **sure?**"

And **Mr Fortesque says,**
"Oh yes, I've been looking for a **brown cat**
as nice as this one for **ages.**"

Mrs Trill looks at **me** and **I** look at **Mrs Trill,**
and we **both** look at my notice,

but neither of us
says a **word.**

I just **love** being a **pet.**

And . . . I am trying to be **really** helpful.

I pick out the best **cheeses**

by using my excellent sniffing nose.

I clean the kitchen

by n i b b l i n g

up the

c r u m b s.

I help Mr Fortesque

I cross the road by **scaring** the traffic.

And I'm **always** there when he comes **home**.

So here I am.

Finally a pet with a name.

So what if I have to wear a little jumper?

Mr Fortesque says, "Well, Tiddles, who's a pretty kittycat?"

And I squeak, "I am!"